Dear Parent:

Congratulations! Your child is taking the first steps on an exciting journey. The destination? Independent reading!

STEP INTO READING® will help your child get there. The program offers five steps to reading success. Each step includes fun stories and colorful art. There are also Step into Reading Sticker Books, Step into Reading Math Readers, Step into Reading Phonics Readers, Step into Reading Write-In Readers, and Step into Reading Phonics Boxed Sets—a complete literacy program with something to interest every child.

Learning to Read, Step by Step!

Ready to Read   Preschool–Kindergarten
• big type and easy words • rhyme and rhythm • picture clues
For children who know the alphabet and are eager to begin reading.

Reading with Help   Preschool–Grade 1
• basic vocabulary • short sentences • simple stories
For children who recognize familiar words and sound out new words with help.

Reading on Your Own   Grades 1–3
• engaging characters • easy-to-follow plots • popular topics
For children who are ready to read on their own.

Reading Paragraphs   Grades 2–3
• challenging vocabulary • short paragraphs • exciting stories
For newly independent readers who read simple sentences with confidence.

Ready for Chapters   Grades 2–4
• chapters • longer paragraphs • full-color art
For children who want to take the plunge into chapter books but still like colorful pictures.

STEP INTO READING® is designed to give every child a successful reading experience. The grade levels are only guides. Children can progress through the steps at their own speed, developing confidence in their reading, no matter what their grade.

Remember, a lifetime love of reading starts with a single step!

For Breanne and Kyle
—K.L.D.

Visit us on the Web!
StepIntoReading.com
randomhousekids.com

Educators and librarians, for a variety of teaching tools, visit us at
RHTeachersLibrarians.com

ISBN: 978-0-307-93032-3 (trade) — ISBN: 978-0-375-97031-3 (lib. bdg.)

Printed in the United States of America
10 9 8 7 6 5

STEP INTO READING®

STEP 2

HERE COMES PETER COTTONTAIL

Adapted by Kristen L. Depken

Illustrated by Linda Karl

Random House 🏠 New York

Easter is coming!
The bunnies
in April Valley
make baskets.
They paint eggs.
They make candy.

The chief Easter bunny
is in charge.

The chief bunny is old.
He asks Peter Cottontail
to be the new chief.
Peter says yes.

Irontail is a mean bunny.

He wants to be chief.

Irontail has a plan.

A contest!

He and Peter will

give out Easter eggs.

The bunny who gives
out more eggs
will be chief.

Irontail gives Peter's
rooster magic gum.
The rooster cannot crow.
Peter sleeps
all day!

Peter does not

give out any eggs.

He loses the contest.

Irontail is
the new chief bunny.
He makes mud eggs
and chocolate spiders.
He ruins Easter!
Peter is sad.
He leaves April Valley.

13

Peter finds
a flying machine.
It flies back
in time!

Peter will go

back to Easter.

He will give out his eggs!

Antoine the pilot helps.

But Irontail's spider
switches the controls
on the flying machine.

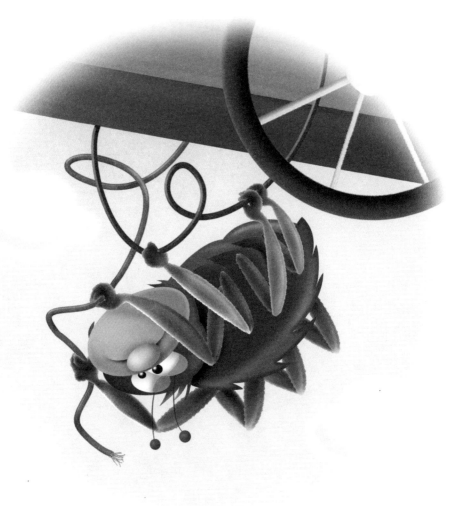

Peter and Antoine

fly the wrong way.

They land

in the Fourth of July!

Peter paints his eggs
red, white, and blue.
Antoine helps.

No one
wants the eggs.

Peter goes
to Halloween next.
He paints his eggs
black and orange.
A witch likes them!

Irontail's pet bat

steals the eggs.

Peter catches them.

Peter goes

to Christmas!

He brings his eggs.

Irontail follows him.

Irontail tries to steal
the eggs!
Santa stops him.
He saves Peter's eggs.

Peter goes

to Valentine's Day.

He paints his eggs.

Peter meets Donna.

He gives her

a red egg.

Peter and Donna
skate together.
They have fun.

Irontail turns

Peter's eggs green!

Donna does not want

green eggs.

Peter flies away.
What will he do
with green eggs?

Peter has a plan.

St. Patrick's Day!

Kids love

his green eggs.

He gives them all away.

Peter wins the contest!
He returns
to April Valley.
Peter's friends
wave and cheer.

31

Peter Cottontail

is the new

chief Easter bunny!